Zorah's Magic Carpet

STEFAN CZERNECKI

For Tony Happy Birthday 98

HYPERION PRESS

CANADA

To Patricia O'Hare Palmer

FIRST EDITION

1   3   5   7   9   10   8   6   4   2

Canadian Cataloguing-in-Publication Data
Czernecki, Stefan, 1946–
Zorah's magic carpet
ISBN 1-895340-06-3
I. Title.
PS8555.Z49Z6 1995   jC813'.54   C95-920026-6
PZ7.C999Zo 1995

The artwork for each picture is prepared using gouache.
This book is set in 14-point Hiroshige.

THINGS DON'T JUST
HAPPEN.
IT DEPENDS ON
WHO COMES ALONG.

Paul Bowles

Long ago a husband and wife named Akhmed and Zorah lived near
the city of Fez in Morocco. Every day Akhmed led his goats to the
hills to graze while Zorah weeded her vegetable garden and took fresh
goat's milk and cheese to the bazaar to sell.

   The bazaar was always crowded with foreign merchants who
came to trade their spices and silks for the local silver jewelry and

finely tooled leather. They would tell stories about distant lands, and Zorah wished that she too could travel the world.

When Akhmed returned home in the evenings with his goats, Zorah always told him about the interesting places of which she had heard and that she wished to visit. Akhmed sipped his sweet mint tea and said he was content to stay where they were.

One day when Akhmed was resting under a tree in the hills near his goats, he saw a lamb that seemed to be lost. Not wanting to leave the poor animal alone, he carried it home, and the couple decided to keep it.

They made a pen for it beside the house, and Zorah fed it warm goat's milk and greens from her garden. The lamb grew quickly, and its coat became thick with soft and silky wool.

In August it was customary for each household to kill a sheep to celebrate the festival of Aïd el-Kabir. Akhmed had never been able to afford a sheep for this special feast day, but now he told Zorah that he would kill their sheep that evening when he returned from the hills. "I am sure it will be a good omen for the coming year," he said.

Zorah took food to the sheep as usual, but when she approached

the pen, the sheep spoke. "Zorah, if you will set me free, I will tell you how you can travel to all the places of which you dream."

Zorah was so startled she couldn't speak.

The sheep continued. "Shear my wool coat, spin it into yarn, dye it the colors of the flowers in the hills, and make a small carpet. Then you shall have your wish."

Zorah sheared the sheep, put the wool in a bag, and opened the gate of the pen so the sheep could escape. That evening when her husband came home, she told him what she had done.

Akhmed was very angry. "The wool cannot be eaten for the feast," he said. "You have been tricked, and since we have no sheep to offer

for the celebration, our luck will not improve."

    Zorah said nothing, but the next day she did what the sheep had said. She spun the wool into yarn, dyed it, set up her loom, and began to weave. The colored fibers seemed to jump from her hands to the loom as an intricate design took shape.

After several months the carpet was finished. Zorah had never made anything so beautiful. The pattern consisted of designs she had seen at the market and represented all the places of which she had dreamed.

Zorah was grateful to the sheep for providing this treasure. Tired

from all her effort, she sat on the carpet to rest.

Immediately it soared into the air. "Stop!" cried Zorah in alarm. The carpet hovered in midair. Zorah thought about what the sheep had said. Then, holding tightly to the edges, she commanded in a loud voice, "Take me to a faraway place." The carpet obeyed at once.

Stepping from the carpet, Zorah looked around and saw the vast Ukraine steppes, or plains. The sun shone brightly, but the chill in the morning air made her shiver. She pulled the carpet around her shoulders and began to walk toward the magnificent city that lay before her.

The gold domes of the great buildings flashed in the sunlight.

Zorah knew the city was Kiev from the stories she had heard.

On the outskirts of the city she stopped at a house to ask permission to drink from the well. When the door opened, she saw that the household was preparing for a wedding. Zorah was invited inside and watched as the women dressed the bride in her embroidered finery.

She wanted to give the bride a gift, so she took off her slippers
and put them on the young woman's feet.

When the singing and dancing began, Zorah wished to join
in but knew she could not stay. Reluctantly she picked up the carpet

and moved toward the door.

    To repay Zorah's kindness, the bride took off her exquisite *vinok*, the traditional wedding headdress, and gave it to the departing guest.

When Akhmed returned from the hills that evening, his wife could not contain her excitement. "I have been on a wonderful adventure," she announced. "I walked across the steppes of Ukraine and visited a city where the buildings have roofs of gold. See what I have brought." She placed the bride's flowered wreath on her head

and pirouetted before her husband.

Akhmed was not impressed. "Zorah," he began, "you must forget this foolishness about traveling. You have not watered the garden nor taken the cheese to the bazaar. How are we to live if you continue to dream all day about far-off places?"

Zorah felt ashamed that she had neglected her work. Many weeks passed, and she ignored the carpet.

Then one day she saw an Indian prince being carried on a palanquin through the crowded stalls of the bazaar. He looked so majestic that Zorah longed to know about his land.

As soon as the cheese was sold, Zorah hurried home, took the carpet into the garden, and said, "Take me to Bombay!"

The carpet took off immediately and set her down in a crowded street, where she was nearly trod upon by a huge elephant.

Zorah walked along looking about her in amazement. Turning a corner, she mistakenly entered a small open doorway. Before her was a garden paradise filled with exotic flowers and birds. At the end of the garden a young woman sat playing a *tanpura*. She motioned to Zorah to sit and listen.

Zorah was enchanted by the music and stayed as long as she dared. When she got up to leave, she took off her silver necklace and placed it around the young woman's neck. In return, the woman gave Zorah a peacock that had been strutting among the flowers.

This time, when Zorah got home, she offered her husband no explanation about her trip. Akhmed was fascinated with the peacock and thought his wife had traded their cheese for it at the bazaar. Every evening when he returned from the hills, he sat in the garden sipping his tea and admiring the handsome bird.

"It gives my eyes great pleasure," he said.

Since Zorah no longer talked about the carpet, Akhmed believed her daydreams were over. "Your carpet is beautiful," he said to her one day. "If I had money to buy sheep, we would have wool to make additional carpets to sell at the bazaar."

Zorah wondered what to do. She knew she could never again make the same design as her carpet, but she could weave other patterns that imitated the bride's flowered wreath and the peacock's fanned tail. No one had such carpets for sale. But where would she get the wool? Needing to think, she said to her carpet, "Take me far away."

The carpet eventually put her down in Beijing, in the midst of the Lantern Festival that celebrates the Chinese New Year. As a huge dragon made of cloth and papier-mâché snaked down the street, onlookers threw firecrackers while colorful fireworks exploded in the air.

"This is truly amazing," Zorah said. She quickly traded her leather bag for fireworks.

When Zorah got home, Akhmed was still in the hills with his goats. Zorah decided to hang her carpet to air while she prepared supper. A rich merchant from the bazaar passed the house. "What a remarkable carpet," he said. "I have never seen such an enchanting pattern. I must have it."

"I can never part with it," Zorah replied. "It shares my dreams."

Then she thought of the fireworks.

"Come with me," she said to the merchant, leading the way into the garden. She lit one of the large sticks, and they watched the bright colors burst in the evening air. "I will sell these instead," she said.

When Akhmed came home that evening, Zorah showed him the gold coins. "Now you can buy the sheep you want," she said, "and I will make fine carpets from the wool."

With the goats and sheep, Akhmed had a large flock. He herded them to the hills every day, and Zorah continued to take goat's milk and cheese to the bazaar.

When she had time, Zorah would go on a journey. She always

returned inspired to create fabulous new designs for her carpets.
Over the years, she wove many beautiful carpets to sell. Each was
admired for its color and unique pattern. But none equaled the original,
which Zorah kept hidden under her bed.

Author's Note

The Berbers were among the first inhabitants of Morocco. In this society that originally traced its descent through the mother rather than the father, women long enjoyed freedom and independence. Traditionally, the Berbers wore elaborate costumes and tattooed their faces and bodies. The women did not wear the veils that were part of Islamic tradition. Gradually influenced by the Arabs and Islam, the Berbers adapted their own culture and traditions, putting their unique stamp on Islamic celebrations and festivals. **Aïd el-Kabir** is one of them. A sheep is slain to commemorate Abraham's near sacrifice of his son Isaac. The performance of the ritual and the feasting are considered good omens for the coming year, and every family tries to participate.

Another important tradition is tea drinking. Strong, sweet mint tea—atai—is central to Berber hospitality. **Bazaars** are also important. These are open-air markets where people gather to buy and sell local produce, woven carpets, tooled leather, and silver jewelry; to bargain for goods from abroad; and to exchange news and arrange marriages.

The **Ukraine steppes** are vast, flat, treeless tracts of land that resemble the prairies of the central United States and Canada. **Kiev** is one of Ukraine's oldest cities. Originally, the onion-shaped domes of its buildings were gold leafed. A **vinok** is an elaborate wreath headdress made from fresh or dried flowers and colored ribbons and worn by brides in Ukraine.

The blue peafowl is the national bird of India. Known to us as the **peacock**, it has magnificent colorful plumage and a fanned tail that can span nine feet in width. It ranges from the foothills of the Himalayan Mountains south to the island of Sri Lanka. The bird is greatly respected in these areas and allowed to walk freely in towns, temples, and gardens.

The **tanpura** is a stringed musical instrument with a long neck that resembles a mandolin.

A **palanquin** is a portable chair for one person, carried on the shoulders of men by means of poles.

The **Lantern Festival**, which celebrates the Chinese New Year, dates back more than two thousand years. On the last day of the festival a mythical dragon appears, symbolizing life forces (vigor, fertility, spring rain). In order for renewal to take place, evil must be driven away. According to legend, evil is represented by a demon named Nian who long ago was locked up in remote mountains by the heavenly god. But Nian escapes every year to do mischief. Luckily he is afraid of noise and the color red. To protect themselves, people used to hang sayings written on red pieces of paper on their gates, build fires, and throw pieces of bamboo on the flames, where they exploded with a bang to scare away Nian.

Later the bamboo pieces were packed with a mixture of ground charcoal and sulfur with an attached fuse. These were reasonably effective as the forerunner to firecrackers. When saltpeter was added to the mixture, a noisy explosion took place—this was the birth of the first firecracker and also the invention of gunpowder. By the sixth century, firecrackers and fireworks were a familiar part of Chinese religious parades and festivals.